LIBRARY OF DOOM

THE FINAL CHAPTERS

THE LOST PAGE

By Michael Dahl

Illustrated by
Nelson Evergreen

Raintree is an imprint of Capstone Global Library Limited, a
company incorporated in England and Wales having its registered
office at 7 Pilgrim Street, London, EC4V 6LB – Registered company
number: 6695582

www.raintree.co.uk
myorders@raintree.co.uk

Designed by Hilary Wacholz
Printed and bound in China by Nordica
0914/CA21401556
ISBN 978-1-4062-9453-8
19 18 17 16 15
10 9 8 7 6 5 4 3 2 1

British Library Cataloguing in Publication Data
A full catalogue record for this book is available from the British
Library.

These are the last days of the Library of Doom.

The forces of villainy are freeing the Library's most dangerous books. Only one thing can stop Evil from penning history's final chapter – the League of Librarians, a mysterious collection of heroes who only appear when the Library faces its greatest threat.

A beautiful cover can hide a hideous evil.

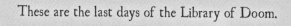

TABLE OF CONTENTS

Chapter 1

BLAST

BOOM!

An explosion **rocks** the Library of Doom!

Dust and smoke roll through the hallways.

Screams echo down the stacks of books and papers.

The young Pages who work there flee in terror!

A deep crater splits the Treasure Vaults of the Library.

The wide hole has blasted through 70 floors.

Dust and smoke boil up from the bottom of the crater.

A tall figure appears in the gloom.

He stands at the **edge** of the top floor.

He gazes down into the deep hole.

It is the Librarian.

Another, younger man appears next to him.

The Red Librarian is dressed in leather the colour of blood.

"One of our Pages is missing," says the Librarian. "Go and search for him while I hunt for whoever did this."

The Red Librarian nods.

Then he steps off the edge of the hole and into the **crater**.

The Red Librarian falls past floor after floor.

Chapter 2

BELOW

The Treasure Vaults hold beautiful, but deadly, volumes.

Books of gold that turn readers to STONE.

Books of jewels so bright that readers are blinded.

The Red Librarian reaches the bottom of the smoky crater.

His boots touch the floor of the cellar.

Piles of books are **heaped** around him.

Clouds of smoke still hang in the air.

In the dim light, the young librarian steps on a book.

It is a book with a **silver** cover.

Webs of gleaming metal spin out of the book.

The webs fly through the air and reach out for the Red Librarian.

The gleaming strands wrap **tightly** around him.

Soon, he is **trapped** in a silver cocoon.

Chapter 3

THE ELDER

A bent shadow moves among the heaps of fallen books.

The shadow moves closer.

It lifts an **ancient** hand.

It points a **wrinkled** finger.

The Red Librarian twists and squirms.

He moves his head from side to side.

A few silver bands move away from his mouth.

"Why did you attack the Library?" asks the hero in red.

The old stranger's eyes grow WIDE.

He bends over, as if he is in pain.

Suddenly, the **dust clouds** part overhead.

The Librarian descends through the gloom.

"Sir!" shouts the red hero. "It's him! The one who blew up the Library!"

The **stranger** gasps.

He raises an arm to protect himself.

"You ... you ..." he stammers.

"Watch out!" shouts the Red Librarian.

Behind the Librarian stands a second figure.

The man wears a uniform of brilliant gems.

Beams flash from the crystals on his uniform.

One of the beams hits a book directly **beneath** the Librarian.

The book has a red gem on its cover.

"Looks like I have you over a beryl!" says the crystal figure with an **EVIL** laugh.

The red gem splits into a dozen jewels.

They spin around the Librarian.

Both Librarians are **trapped**.

Chapter 4

THE TOPAZ OF TIME

"Watch-Man!" shouts the Librarian.

"Exactly," says the gleaming figure. "And now my Topaz of Time will cause you to grow **older**. Just as I made the floors of the library grow old and weak."

"It was an implosion," explains the ancient man. "Not an explosion."

The Watch-Man points to the old one. "That is your young Page, Librarian. Now old and lost."

"The floors above you grew old and **crumbled**," adds the Watch-Man. "Watch your Page grow older and die!"

"No!" shouts the Red Librarian, as he throws himself into the deadly beam of light.

The light bounces off the silver cocoon.

The reflected beam shines onto the Watch-Man.

His Topaz ages a thousand years and turns to sparkling dust.

A huge rumble fills the air.

One by one, the floors above them rise back into place.

Books fly back onto their shelves.

The clouds of dust dissolve around them.

"Thanks, Librarian," says the Page, returned to his younger self.

"Don't thank me," says the Librarian. He points to the scarlet hero. "When you need a hero who knows the Library, call on someone who is, well, red."

GLOSSARY

ancient – very, very old

beryl – type of mineral that is usually green or blueish green but can also be white, blue, yellow or red

crater – large hole in the ground made by an explosion or something that fell

dissolve – disappear slowly, fade away

implosion – act of falling or bursting inwards

page – young person who works as a helper or as a servant for someone

topaz – type of mineral that is a clear yellow or brown but can also be colourless, blue or pink

volume – one book of a series of books

DISCUSSION QUESTIONS

1. Why do you think the Watch-Man broke into the Treasure Vaults? What was he looking for?

2. Who do you think is stronger: the Librarian, the Red Librarian or the Watch-Man? Explain your answer.

3. The Librarian needed Red to help him on his mission. Who are some people that you help? Who helps you?

WRITING PROMPTS

1. The Watch-Man wears a uniform of magical gems. Write a paragraph describing what your uniform would look like if you were a superhero or villain.

2. Besides the silver book, what other dangerous things were kept in the Treasure Vaults? Write down at least three other valuable but deadly books that were stored there. What are their powers?

3. The Red Librarian had his special colour. Do you have a favourite colour? Write down what it is and explain why you like it.

THE AUTHOR

Michael Dahl is the prolific author of the bestselling *Goodnight, Baseball* picture book and more than 200 other books for children and young adults. He has won the AEP Distinguished Achievement Award three times for his non-fiction, a Teachers' Choice Award from *Learning* magazine and a Seal of Excellence from the Creative Child Awards. He is also the author of the Hocus Pocus Hotel mysteries and the Dragonblood series. Dahl currently lives in Minneapolis, Minnesota, USA.

THE ILLUSTRATOR

Nelson Evergreen lives on the south coast of England with his partner and their imaginary cat. Evergreen is a comics artist, illustrator and general all-round doodler of whatever nonsense pops into his head. He contributes regularly to the UK underground comics scene, and is currently writing and illustrating a number of graphic novel and picture book hybrids for older children.